Nothing Ever Happens on 90th Street

by Roni Schotter

illustrated by Kyrsten Brooker

Orchard Books
New York

Eva unwrapped a cinnamon Danish, opened her notebook, and stared helplessly at the wide, white pages. "Write about what you know," her teacher, Mrs. DeMarco, had told her. So Eva sat high on the stoop and looked out over 90th Street waiting for something to happen. A horn honked. A radio rapped. A kid cried. The usual. "Nothing ever happens on 90th Street," Eva scribbled in her notebook.

A few doors down, Mr. Chang was arranging fish fillets in his newly opened Seafood Emporium. No one was buying, and his shop looked as empty and ignored as the tiny, boarded-up store next door to it. He nodded to a woman passing by and called hello to Eva.

Out the door of Eva's building came Mr. Sims, the actor, carrying his enormous cat, Olivier. Mr. Sims was "on hiatus again," which meant out of work, in between shows, and so, every day, dressed in his finest, he embarked on a daily promenade with Olivier under his arm. "Writing?" he asked.

"Trying to," Eva answered, "but nothing ever happens on 90th Street!"

"You are mistaken, my dear," Mr. Sims said. "The whole world's a stage — even 90th Street — and each of us plays a part. Watch the stage, observe the players carefully, and don't neglect the details," he said, stroking Olivier. "Follow an old actor's advice and you will find you have plenty to write about."

"Thanks," Eva said, and fast as she could, using as many details as she could recall, Eva described Mr. Sims in her notebook—his felt fedora hat, his curly gray hair, his shiny button shoes. When she looked up, he was halfway down the street and Mr. Morley, the mousse maker, was at his window.

Just as he did every day, Mr. Morley set his chocolate pot and coffee urn out on his ledge with a sign. Mr. Morley dreamed of having a catering business where the fanciest people demanded his dessert. But the trouble was . . . Mr. Morley's mousse was missing something. No matter how he tried, his mousse never had much taste, and Mr. Morley never had many customers.

"Writing?" he asked.

"Um. Hmmm," Eva answered, chewing on her pencil.

"Try to find the poetry in your pudding," Mr. Morley said softly. "There's always a new way with old words."

"You're right," Eva said, wishing Mr. Morley would one day find the poetry in *his* pudding. Taking his advice, she tried to think up a new way to describe the look of Mr. Morley's mousse. Smooth and dark as midnight. Or maybe more like mink! Yes, that was it! Eva thought, writing in her notebook.

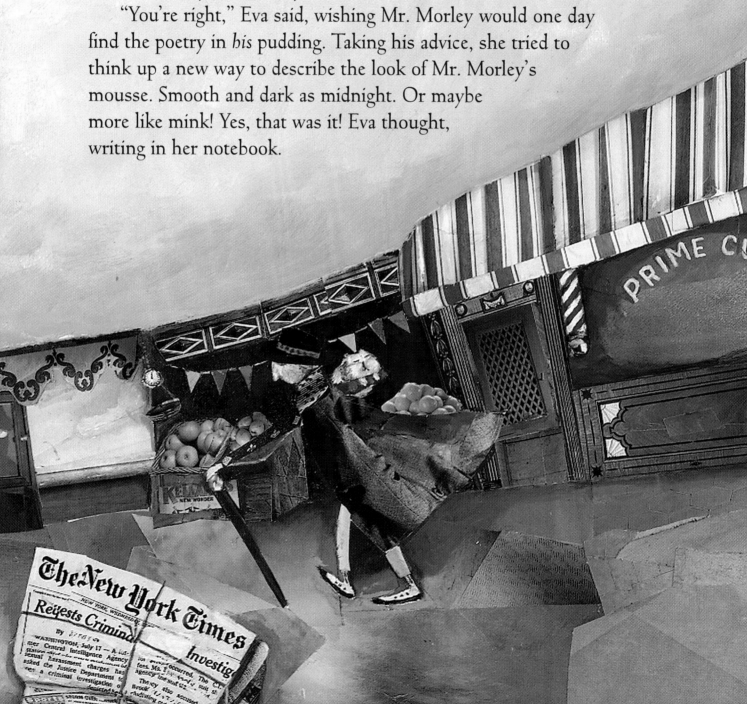

The door to the building slammed and a gust of wind sent dead leaves soaring and dipping like crazy kites. Alexis Leora nodded to Eva and stepped gracefully down the steps to do her warm-up exercises. Alexis was a dancer. When she wanted to, she could hold an extremely long leg straight up against her ear like a one-legged woman with three arms. But she couldn't smile. Eva decided it was because Alexis Leora was lonely.

"Writing?" Alexis Leora asked Eva.

"Yes," Eva answered.

Alexis Leora did six deep knee bends and then sighed. "Stretch," she said sadly. "Use your imagination. If your story doesn't go the way you want it to, you can always stretch the truth. You can ask, 'What if?' and make up a better story."

"You're right," Eva said, thinking "What if?" What if Alexis Leora met someone? Would she smile then? What would that look like? Eva closed her eyes to try to picture it, but all she could picture was soup — Spanish soup — rich and brown and so spicy it seemed as if she could actually smell it.

She could! When Eva opened her eyes, Mrs. Martinez was standing beside her. She nodded to Alexis Leora as she handed Eva a bowl of soup. "Have some," she said. "Writers *need* soup. What's your story about?"

"Nothing much." Eva sighed. "Nothing ever happens on 90th Street."

"Add a little action," Mrs. Martinez said. "Like soup. A little this. A little that. And don't forget the spice. Mix it. Stir it. Make something happen. Surprise yourself!" She nodded again to Alexis Leora and went inside.

Eva put down her pencil and tasted Mrs. Martinez's wonderful, surprising soup. She thought about her story. It wasn't wonderful. It wasn't surprising. But what could she do? Nothing ever happened on 90th Street. How could she possibly "add a little action" and "make something happen"? Eva had no ideas. She was stuck!

Then Mrs. Friedman from up the block came wheeling Baby Joshua in his stroller. He was holding a bright red ball in two tiny, fat hands. "Bird!" he called out to a pigeon hunting for something to eat. "Bird. Hungry!"

"Pigeon," Mrs. Friedman told him.

Eva sighed and looked down at her half-eaten Danish, then at her notebook. She looked at Baby Joshua, then at the pigeon. She remembered Alexis Leora's words of advice. "What if?" Eva thought. Suddenly she had an idea.

What if she stood up, broke her Danish into dozens of tiny pieces, and scattered them wide and wild into the street? What would happen? Eva laughed to think of it. . . .

From lampposts and ledges dozens of pigeons swooped down to dine on Danish. Eva eagerly picked up her pencil and began to write again. "Bird!" Baby Joshua called out, pointing. "More bird!" he cried, panting. The bright red ball dropped out of his tiny, fat hands and bounced onto the sidewalk. "Bye, bye, ball!" Baby Joshua screamed.

The ball rolled off the curb, into the street, and straight into the path of a pizza delivery man on his bicycle!

Everyone gasped in horror. Alexis Leora paused in mid-plié and leaped to the rescue. She got there just as the pizza delivery man landed, right side up, at her feet. Alexis Leora looked down at the pizza man and he looked up at her. And then something almost unimaginable happened: Alexis Leora smiled! "Are y-y-you all right?" she asked, shyly. Her smile was sweet and bright. Her teeth were straight and white. (It was the first time Eva or anyone on 90th Street had seen them!)

"Yes," said the pizza man, smiling up at her. It was love at first sight. Pepperoni and peppers rained down on the happy couple. The pizza man pulled a pepper out of his hair as horns began to honk.

Eva added this to her notebook and wondered what could possibly happen next. . . .

A long, white limousine was honking its horn loudest of all. The limo driver rolled down his window. "Whad'ya wanna block traffic for?" he called out. The back door of the limo opened and out stepped a woman in sunglasses, wearing a turban and a coat the color of a taxi.

"There seems to be a problem, Henry," she said in a fake English accent. "There's some sort of accident here. Perhaps—"

"It's *Sondra!*" someone suddenly screamed, interrupting her. "Sondra! Can I have your autograph?" Mrs. Martinez called out.

"Sondra Saunderson!" Mr. Morley blushed.

Was Eva dreaming? There, in the middle of 90th Street, larger than life, stood Sondra Saunderson, star of stage, screen, and the sensational soap opera "One World To Live In."

"Darlings, what's happening here? I'm sure I . . . *Lar-ry!*" she called out suddenly, and stretched her arms toward Mr. Sims, who had just returned from his promenade. "It's been an age since we saw each other!"

Mr. Sims' cat, about to be crushed in an extravagant embrace, leaped out of Mr. Sims' arms to chase after Baby Joshua's ball.

"Olivier!" Mr. Sims called out. "Come back!"

Everyone raced into the street after the ball, but it was the limo driver who, in the right place at the right time, leaned into the gutter and picked it up.

With a flick of the wrist, he tossed the ball to Mrs. Friedman, who presented it to a drooling but grateful Baby Joshua.

"How's that for a throw?" the limo driver proudly asked the crowd.

No one, not even Baby Joshua, had a chance to answer. Olivier, frightened by so many people, raced past Eva, scrambled onto Mr. Morley's ledge, where he knocked over his coffee urn, spilling all the coffee into his mousse pot.

"Ruined!" Mr. Morley cried, wringing his hands.

At that, Olivier bounded to the top of a ginkgo tree, where he swayed dangerously like a heavy, white balloon.

"Now he'll *never* come down!" Mr. Sims lamented. "He's terribly stubborn."

"There, there, Larry," Sondra Saunderson comforted him. "I'm sure someone on 90th Street will have a solution."

Eva tried to imagine who that could possibly be. . . .

"I have one!" she heard Mr. Chang call out. Generously, he offered trout, fresh from his store, to Olivier.

High up in the tree, Olivier barely blinked.

"Raw trout?" Mr. Sims sighed. "My regrets, Mr. Chang. He won't eat it. He's a *gourmet* cat. I'm afraid I've spoiled him. Whatever will I do?"

"What if?" Eva asked herself for the second time that day, and suddenly she had another idea. A truly great one! She whispered it to Mr. Morley, Mrs. Martinez, and Mr. Chang.

"Brilliant!" Mr. Morley exclaimed. And with that he, Mrs. Martinez, and Mr. Chang, still clutching his trout, vanished into the building.

Eva righted Mr. Morley's coffee urn and stuck her finger into his ruined mousse, then into her mouth to determine the degree of damage. "Mocha!" she called out in surprise. "Mr. Morley's mousse is mocha now and . . ." She paused, trying to find the perfect word. "*Magnificent!*" she announced to the assembled throng. And, giving the pot a stir, she dished out samples to all assembled.

"Delicious!" Alexis Leora said, spooning some into the pizza man's mouth.

"Poetry!" Sondra Saunderson pronounced.

Now on 90th Street, people who had never spoken to one another before were speaking at last. The pizza delivery man and the limo driver shook hands, and everyone tried to tempt Olivier down from his precarious perch.

And then . . . Mr. Morley appeared on the steps, followed by Mrs. Martinez and Mr. Chang. Mrs. Martinez carried a large pot of her surprising soup, while Mr. Morley carried a platter of Mr. Chang's trout, now surrounded by many tiny vegetables and cooked to perfection. With the addition of a cup of Mr. Morley's cat-created mocha mousse—it was a meal worthy of the finest culinary establishment.

"Do you smell that, Olivier?" Mr. Sims called, fanning the steam so it rose up the ginkgo tree.

Olivier took one deep sniff and bolted down the tree to dine!

Everyone on 90th Street sampled each course and everyone on 90th Street sighed with delight. "Superb!" "*Fantastico!*" "Yum!"

Eva smiled and glanced up from her notebook. For the third time that day she asked herself, "What if?"

"Mr. Chang," she began, "you and Mr. Morley and Mrs. Martinez are such great cooks. The boarded-up store next to your Seafood Emporium, what if all of you used it for a restaurant?"

"A restaurant?" The three chefs looked at one another. "What a wonderful idea," they said, shaking Eva's hand. "Everyone on 90th Street could be our customers. You too, Sondra."

"Everyone but me," Mr. Sims said regretfully. "Just now, I'm between jobs and a bit low on cash."

"No longer!" Sondra called out. "You'll be on my show! I'll arrange it."

Mr. Sims kissed Sondra's hand, and everyone cheered.

"What an amazing day!" Mrs. Martinez said. "Who would believe it? If only someone had written it all down."

"I did," Eva announced, and she opened her notebook and began to read her story (the same story you're reading now) about how *nothing* ever happened on 90th Street.

"What a story!" Sondra exclaimed. "Full of detail. Dialogue. Suspense. A bit of poetry. A hint of romance. Even a happy ending. Why, you'd almost think some of it was made up!"

Eva smiled mysteriously. "Thanks," she said proudly. "But just wait. It'll be even better . . . after I rewrite it."

For my dear friends on 90th Street
Diane, Joel, Evan, & Rachel Silverman
and
Lee Wallace & Marilyn Chris Wallace —R.S.

For Mom and Dad —K.B.

Text copyright © 1997 by Roni Schotter

Illustrations copyright © 1997 by Kyrsten Brooker

Orchard Books
95 Madison Avenue
New York, NY 10016

Manufactured in the United States of America
Printed by Barton Press, Inc.   Bound by Horowitz/Rae
Book design by Chris Hammill Paul

10   9   8   7   6   5   4   3   2   1

The text of this book is set in 17 point Truesdell.   The illustrations are collage.

Library of Congress Cataloging-in-Publication Data
Schotter, Roni.
    Nothing ever happens on 90th Street / by Roni Schotter ; illustrated by Kyrsten Brooker.
        p.   cm.
    "A Melanie Kroupa book" — Half t.p.
    Summary: When Eva sits on her stoop trying to complete a school assignment by writing about what
happens in her neighborhood, she gets a great deal of advice and action.
    ISBN 0-531-09536-3. — ISBN 0-531-08886-3 (lib. bdg.)
    [1. Authorship — Fiction. 2. Neighborliness — Fiction.]
I. Brooker, Kyrsten, ill. II. Title.
PZ7.S3765Np   1997
[Fic] — dc20
                                                                                          96-4000